The Office
Nutter

The Office Nutter

Elena Kavin

Nicollette Little, copy editor
Catarina Oliveira, cover illustration
David Moratto, cover production and interior design

First edition
Printed in Canada

ISBN: 978-1-7773818-0-6 (print)
ISBN: 978-1-7773818-1-3 (ebook)

Dedicated to my beloved son

Signature Marissa Moments

Meet Marissa

Marissa has been employed with us for about 12 years. She is undoubtedly a hard-working, competent employee with a broad knowledge of the luxury home decor industry. But there is more. Much, much more — so stay tuned...

Marissa is a woman who waddles through life, convinced that she is one of God's select and perfect creations, and most certainly, the saviour of our company.

She occupies a large office with a glass door, overlooking the technical support team. She sits behind an oversized desk that is covered with piles of paperwork, documents and samples. Although our company has a clear 'green policy', Marissa still prints every single email and document sent to her, then 'files' them in one of the many stacks on her desk or floor, or on any vacant surface. There are six guest chairs in her office. If you need to confer with her, however, be prepared to do so standing up: every chair is 'occupied' by mountains of paper. Nonetheless, when you ask her a question regarding a product or customer, she knows exactly in which of the many piles lies the answer, complete with dates, time stamps and names.

The office cleaner, Sadie, has long given up on any attempt to dust that desk, or hoover the scant vacant space on the carpet, for fear of knocking down a tower of paper. She still remembers being yelled at for slightly moving one of those stacks on a dark afternoon. Sadie came to see me, tears in her eyes, fearful that she might lose her job. I promised her that this particular office would no longer be part of her routine.

When you walk past Marissa's office, you can barely see her amidst the insane clutter. You can, however, hear her pounding mercilessly on the poor keyboard, using only her index fingers. We had to purchase a new keyboard for her each year. All the broken ones are kept in a large box in the stock room, marked in red block letters: "**WORK CASUALTIES.**"

The office temperature has always been a bone of contention for the team. Most find it too cold, but not Marissa. We finally all agreed to maintain a comfortable and steady 22 degrees Celsius. Marissa suffers from intense hot flashes, so she keeps a small fan on her desk that blows directly at her face, full speed, all day long.

Barely five feet tall, she can often be heard stomping

down the hallway, supporting her short and squat body with her astonishingly large feet, as she makes her way towards the thermostat. Always suspicious that one of us is 'out to get her', she conducts daily inspections of the office temperature. Armed with Scotch Tape, she makes sure that the sign affixed above the thermostat is there to stay. "**DO NOT TOUCH!**" it reads. Imagine the reaction of the technician who comes for yearly maintenance of the system...

Marissa is obsessively devoted to snacking: a habit that has yielded her a compounding 10-pound padding gain year after year. Her lunch bag is practically a full-sized backpack. At any given time, there is a large bowl of snacks on her desk: fruit, nuts and the occasional chocolate. For the most part, it's all very healthy—but the quantities could feed an entire team.

Her piercing beady eyes hold a permanent expression of intense annoyance: one that can easily rattle even the bravest of soldiers. Her lips speak her unfiltered mind, bluntly and without discrimination or discernment. On more than one occasion, she's brought a teammate to tears. The stronger ones just laugh it off: it's another one for the books!

Do you get the picture?

Want to have a real chuckle? Read on...

A Case of Brumotactillophobia

One of **Marissa's** numerous quirks is a severe case of Brumotactillophobia. Naturally, you would wonder what the heck this is. I understand, as I can barely pronounce it myself.

In lay terms, it is a fear of food touching—a form of obsessive-compulsive disorder. OK, I know, phobias are hardly a laughing matter and many of us have at least one. Marissa, being Marissa, however, has quite a few.

I was aware to some extent of this particular phobia, as teammates would sometimes joke about her frantic reactions during lunch. Since I rarely lunched with the team, I had not experienced this displeasure personally. At least, not until one infamous evening...

Marissa and I were attending a conference out of town and had arranged to meet for dinner.

Choosing a restaurant was, by itself, a total ordeal. I was

tired and had a lot on my mind, so picking a fight with her over it was not an option. I decided to just go with her flow.

The main street offered various eateries, from fine cuisine to family restaurants. Marissa insisted on visiting numerous ones, scanning each menu carefully and looking inside each restaurant. Exhausted, I sat on a bench and waited for her to complete each inspection.

Most inspections failed immediately: the restaurant was not clean enough, there were too many children, the menu options were limited, the food looked unappealing, it was loud, and on and on. Each inspection concluded with a look of disgust on her face.

After the sixth restaurant was written off, I'd had enough. "For fuck's sake, Marissa, it's just dinner. We don't need to write a thesis about it, so just choose one and let's get it over with."

She knew me well enough than to push further, so we went into a steak restaurant. Although I am not a fan of beef, I knew she loved it. Surely, I figured, I can find something else on the menu and, in any case, I'd already lost what little appetite I had.

After a 20-minute wait, the waiter showed us to an available table, but of course Marissa did not approve. The restaurant was packed, a line-up of people waiting to get in, and Marissa insisted on the one table that had yet to be cleaned. I looked at the poor waiter and rolled my eyes.

He immediately understood that it was best not to argue. I'll have to tip the poor bugger handsomely, I thought to myself.

We finally sat down and Marissa studied the menu. Her glasses at the tip of her nose and her facial expressions, accompanied by an occasional sound of annoyance, were warning signs of her next move. "Buckle up," I told myself, "and do not engage." And, I was right.

The waiter approached us, but she waived him off. "I am not ready yet. Give me a few minutes."

He remained composed and polite, and I smiled at him, trying to loosen the tense atmosphere.

Ten minutes later, he was back. "Good evening, ladies. My name is Eric and I will be your server. Are you ready to order, Miss?" he asked.

"I think so, but I have a few questions first," Marissa said. Well, of course she would!

"How is the New York Strip prepared?"

"It is one of our most popular cuts, Miss."

"That's not what I asked," she sneered at him.

"I know, Miss, I wasn't finished. It is marinated over-night and grilled to your liking, rare, med..."

He couldn't even complete the sentence, as she jumped in again: "I don't like it rare!"

"OK, how do you like your steak, Miss?"

"Medium, not a drop of blood in the centre."

"Not a probl..."

Again, she cut him off. He kept on looking at me, his eyes begging me to come to his rescue.

"What side dishes come with it?"

"Mashed potatoes, fries or rice pilaf, and today's vegetables are a medley of roasted beets and grilled portobello mushrooms."

"Mushrooms?" she screeched. "Disgusting, no mushrooms for me. Now, listen to me please: Make sure to tell the chef that my food cannot touch under any circumstances, or I won't be able to eat it. Do you understand?"

"Yes, Miss, I will mention it to the chef. Would you like a starter as well?"

"No, nothing looks good. Just the meal and some bread."

At that point the poor guy looked exasperated. He was young, possibly a student doing this job part time. Boy, will he have a story to tell tonight, I thought.

He turned to me. "How about you, Miss? What will you have?"

"The scallops, please, all sides and, most importantly, no special instructions for the chef."

I winked at him and he finally smiled, relieved.

By the time Marissa's meal had arrived, she had already consumed two dinner rolls packed with butter.

"Are you not eating any bread?" she asked, not out of interest, of course, but merely to check if she could chow down the last remaining bun.

"No bread for me."

The waiter approached our table with small, hesitant steps, carrying two plates. He placed mine, and I responded, "Thank you, Eric. This looks really good." He then slowly lowered Marissa's plate to the table. "Enjoy your meal, ladies," he said, turning around swiftly and hoping to make a run for it.

Sadly, he wasn't fast enough.

"OH, MY GOD, OH, MY GOD, I CAN'T EAT THIS! TAKE IT AWAY. TAKE IT AWAY NOW!" Marissa got up, stood away from the table and pointed at the plate with a dreadful expression on her face.

Poor Eric hurried back, expecting the absolute worst: a hair in the food, perhaps a bug...

Other diners turned their heads to look at us, some looking genuinely concerned by Marissa's frantic reaction. I could see some inspecting their own plates for fear of something really horrible nesting in their food.

Eric looked at her plate, puzzled.

"What seems to be the problem, Miss?"

"Look, look, there is a piece of mushroom here. I told you I don't eat mushrooms. And look, the beet is touching the beef. Oh, gross! It left a red mark on the beef. I told you that my food can't touch. Take it away, quickly! I can't bear to look at it!" She waved her hands over the plate as if she were shooing away a pet.

She was shaking and her glasses fogged up. She wiped

them dry and put them back on, only to notice everyone around her staring. Some were laughing, while others whispered. A young mother tried to distract her little boy, who seemed genuinely scared of the crazy old lady. What a bloody unnecessary and embarrassing ordeal.

"But I told him, I clearly told him that my food can't touch. And that disgusting mushroom...I told him, you heard me."

I was too startled by what I had just witnessed to respond. I guess she was hoping for empathy, but all I could manage was, "What the fuck?"

For a moment I thought she was having a nervous breakdown, but no, her reactions are always dramatic and disturbing. So, I chose to ignore it and her. In times like these, less is best, and there's no point engaging in futile attempts to reason.

I got up and pulled Eric aside. He looked as though he had just been punched in the stomach, or worse.

"I am so very sorry and this in no way reflects on you, the chef or the restaurant. She is a fucking nutcase. I am so embarrassed. Please pack my plate to go and you can discard hers. I will of course pay for both. I'm really sorry you had to witness this."

"Thank you, Miss. Wow. I just started this job a few days ago, and, honestly, as of five minutes ago, I was going to quit tonight."

"I understand. It's enough to traumatize most people.

Lucky for you, you won't ever see her again. I, on the other hand, still have to work with her! I hope you can take some comfort in it."

He chuckled with relief.

"Hey, at least you have a good story to tell your friends over beers, time and time again. The more you tell it, the funnier it will seem."

"Yeh, but who'd believe me?"

"Ask around. Someone must have captured it on their phone. I won't be surprised if it shows up online by morning," I laughed.

"OK, let's settle the bill now," I said. I touched his shoulder lightly, thinking that he must be my daughter's age. "Thanks for your patience, Eric," I continued, as I handed him a generous, well-deserved tip.

I walked back to our table only to see Marissa devouring yet another dinner roll loaded with butter.

"Get ready to go, Marissa. I took care of the bill. Time to leave."

"But what about my dinner? I am still hungry. This wasn't my fault!" she screeched.

"Seriously, you still want to eat here? Do as you please, but I just lost my appetite and I am out of here. In the future you might consider carrying your own kiddie's divided plate to a restaurant to avoid another scene."

She was clearly unhappy with my lack of support, but she got up reluctantly and followed. As we made our way out of the crowded restaurant, she noticed the many disapproving faces, all looking happy to see us leave. It felt like the ultimate walk of shame!

We returned to the hotel after the longest 10-minute walk I've ever had, the whole time in pure silence. I tend to walk quickly, but Marissa waddles. Under different circumstances, I would have made an effort and adjusted my pace to hers, but not that night. I carried on full speed and, yes, took pleasure in her panting and desperate struggle to catch up.

"Do you have to walk so fast?" she huffed, adding, "We're in no hurry?"

I didn't bother to respond. By the time we reached the hotel, her face glistened with sweat beads.

I walked over to bar and ordered a needed and well-deserved Martini!

3

The Elevator Incident

Another three-day-long conference with Marissa. How bloody exciting [sigh…]. A mix up with our reservation landed us with lovely room upgrades on the 20th floor, overlooking the marina. Perhaps this won't be so bad after all…

Marissa's room is next to mine. We have arranged for her to knock on my door when she is ready to head downstairs for the cocktail reception hosted by our customer.

The thought of food always excites Marissa: It's been barely 10 minutes and already there is a knock on the door. Fuck!

"Are you ready? I am starving!" she says.

"How can you be starving? Didn't you eat on the flight?" It's a redundant question, of course. She sat next to me and I watched her devour her meal.

"What can I say? I am still a little hungry. The food on the plane was not so good."

I grab my purse and we head towards the elevator.

I notice four different posters near the elevator, each detailing a different conference taking place at the hotel, including the one we are attending. I expect the lobby will be very busy.

The elevator ride is long, stopping at every floor. By the time we reach the 16th, there are a dozen of us on board. The door opens and three ladies are about to step in when it happens...

Marissa steps forward and—with her short arms outstretched and a frantic look on her face—blocks the doors.

Oh shit, here we go again...

The elevator's other passengers' glance at each other, trying to figure out what's going on. The three ladies also stand by the doors, wondering what on earth is happening, when Marissa screeches in a high-pitched voice: "You can't come in! There are too many of us and I am claustrophobic. Please wait for the next elevator."

A man in the elevator points to the sign on the wall and reads aloud: "Maximum 24 passengers. There are about a dozen of us here. No reason these ladies can't join."

"Thank you, sir," said one of the ladies. "The elevator took so long to arrive with the hotel fully booked. We're running late as it is."

She takes a step forward and Marissa goes into hysterics. She's scaring the shit out of the poor ladies.

"But you don't understand!" Marissa shrieks: "I am

claustrophobic. They can't come in!" Her face has broken into a sweat and she's removed her glasses. The passengers all seem uncomfortable. One guy repeatedly checks his watch, appearing particularly agitated.

I take her arm and drag her out of the elevator.

"Excuse us, ladies. The elevator is all yours," I say. They nod and slowly walk past Marissa. They're probably afraid of triggering another outburst.

"What are you doing?" she screams. "We were here first! Why should they go ahead of us?"

"Marissa, for fuck's sake, you cannot control the elevator. We are on the 20th floor, the hotel is fully booked, the elevators need to run at full capacity — and you can't shoo people away."

"So, what am I supposed to do? You know I am claustrophobic."

"Actually, no, I didn't know that. Still, it is your issue to deal with, and you can't drag innocent strangers into this."

"How do you suppose I do this? What are you, a doctor?"

"You can take the stairs. Go to reception and see if by chance they can give you a room on the ground floor."

"Take the stairs? Are you out of your mind? Me, walk 20 flights of stairs? Why should I give up my room? I like my room. What's wrong with you?"

"What's wrong with me, Marissa? Seriously? Look, we are on the 16th floor now. It shouldn't be so hard and its easier to go down the stairs than to climb up. Alternatively, you can wait for the next elevator, and the next, and the next, and hope that one of them won't be full, but I wouldn't count on it."

I pressed the button for the elevator and a long two minutes later the door opened. I walked in, then turned around and I saw her hesitating. The doors were closing when I heard her exasperated voice, "I guess I will take the stairs."

As the elevator doors shut, I burst out laughing. The group of guests looked at me curiously, smiling. "You had to be there," I said.

The cocktail reception was in full swing. I headed to the bar and ordered a much-needed Vodka Martini and proceeded to mingle with the many familiar faces.

"Oh, hi, so nice to see you again," said Mr. Crane, one of our customers. "Wasn't Marissa joining you?"

"Oh, hey, Mr. Crane, good to see you. Marissa should be here shortly."

About 30 minutes later, I spotted Marissa entering the hall. She looked like a defeated soldier right off of a battlefield. I thought it best to leave her be for a time and tried to blend in with the crowd. Despite my attempt to avoid her, if only for a few minutes, there she was, right next to me.

Her freshly blow-dried hair was now wet and pressed against her scalp, and her forehead was covered in sweat beads. I reached into my purse and handed her a pack of Kleenex.

"Oh, thank you, I got all sweaty. Is it really bad? Does it show?"

"No, it does not. Don't worry about it," I replied. White lies are necessary sometimes, if only to keep the peace.

"I spoke to reception. Someone will get my suitcase for me. They gave me a room on the second floor."

"Ok, it's good they were able to accommodate you. So, problem resolved, right?"

Wrong.

"Well, they gave me a handicap room with bars all over the place and the room smells of cheap aftershave. I really liked the room on the 20th floor!"

Oh boy, I thought to myself.

"Good, then you can take the stairs no problem, right?"

"I guess so," she muttered.

4

Entomophobic Panic Attack

Stephanie, our receptionist, has just advised me that the caterer has arrived and is setting up in the boardroom. An important meeting is about to take place. We've landed a lucrative account. Everyone is excited, and, being a hunter by nature, I am at my best today. The project's timeline is ambitious and decisions must be made quickly and accurately. The president herself, accompanied by her two senior vice presidents, are in attendance.

I gather my team at my office for a final brief before we head to the boardroom. Everyone is on board for today's mission, which is to wow and excite the client. Off we go.

The caterer outdid herself once again and everything looks delicious. It seems the president is a real foodie, savouring every bite with an approving nod and an occasional smile. "This is absolutely lovely. Please make sure to leave your business card with me," she tells the caterer. Then she turns to me and says, "That was very kind of you. We appreciate it." Clearly, she's a classy lady. We are going to get along just fine.

The creative team begins the presentation and it goes well. In fact, it's flawless. I observe the reactions around the room, and everyone seems engaged.

The president is impressed. She stands up and walks to the board. "May I?" she asks, as she proceeds to move some items around, then steps back, now completely satisfied. "There! What do you think everyone? Do you get the vision?"

Roland, our creative director, seems especially pleased, since this was his original idea. The president's marketing VP says, "ladies and gentlemen, this is fine work indeed. You really captured the essence of this project. Congratulations and thank you."

We pulled it off and I'm so proud of my team. We must celebrate tonight; I think to myself. I will take them out for a well-deserved meal.

Roland, however, has one final suggestion. "If I may, there is one more version we would like to share. The item was held at Customs, but reception has just advised me it's arrived. Marissa, would you please retrieve it? I believe it was delivered to your office?"

"Sure, Roland. I will be right back."

There is much excitement in the room and the president shares with us some of the back-end efforts to which we weren't privy prior to this meeting. We have clearly earned her full confidence.

Roland and the VP marketing are again by the board doing what they do best, being creative; the caterer is placing desert and coffee on the table; and the president is enjoying little bites of the pastries when suddenly we all hear screams. These screams are followed by, "Oh, my God! Oh, my God!" and then a loud thump, like a heavy object hitting the ground. Everyone stops talking. The president's coffee has spilled all over the table. Roland has grabbed some napkins and is frantically trying to prevent the coffee from running onto her dress.

"Excuse me. Please carry on," I say, as I run out of the boardroom expecting the worst. Tony is standing at reception, and our tech team's members are laughing. What the hell is going on, and today of all days, I think to myself.

Tony takes my arm and whispers, "It's Marissa."

"Is she OK? Is she hurt?"

"Hurt is a relative word. You'd better see for yourself."

We walk towards her office only to find her crouched on her desk, tears running down her face, a large FedEx box on the ground along with a few smaller boxes, an industrial stapler and a broken mug.

"What is going on? Are you hurt?"

Her voice trembles as she kneels on the desk and points to the ground. "There, there...it's hiding over there."

"What are you pointing at, the FedEx box?" I ask.

"Under the box, look under the box," she screams.

Tony lifts the box, but nothing's there. He picks up the other boxes, the stapler and a pair of scissors, but still, there's nothing at all.

"My God, it escaped. It must still be here. You must find it!"

"What is it, Marissa? What are we looking for?"

"There was a huge bug on the floor. A disgusting bug. Please find it! I can't leave the office until someone finds it."

I look at Tony in total disbelief, but he just rolls his eyes. I get the impression he's gotten used to these kinds of outbursts. He seems relaxed and composed.

"A little bug? Are you fucking kidding me? All this commotion for a small bug and today of all days? Everyone heard your screams all the way to the boardroom. We thought someone was being attacked!"

"It was not small. It was huge, black and hairy."

I turned around to leave her office only to find our guests all standing outside the boardroom, looking concerned and very, very perplexed. Fuck, they must have heard us. What will they think of us now?

"Tony, please, would you deal with the little fucker?"

"Marissa or the bug?" asks Tony, who was always helpful and funny.

"Both," I reply with a wink.

"It's not the first time this has happened," he tells me. "The last time, two weeks ago, you were out of town. We heard her screaming, then she ran out of the office and hid in her car. I let her sit there for a good twenty minutes, then walked over with an old squished Kleenex in my hand and told her I killed it. Between us, there was nothing in the Kleenex, but I knew she wouldn't want to see any 'evidence' anyways."

"Thank you, Tony. Now let's work on some damage control."

"I am so very sorry, everyone. We have everything under control, so let's return to the boardroom." It was, of course, challenging to convince them of this, what with Marissa still kneeling on her desk.

I offered a vague explanation, hoping to just make it all go away. The caterer handed me a cup of coffee, but what I really needed was a Martini. I wondered what was going on in their minds, having just witnessed this most bizarre incident — by a key player on the team, no less!

The 'frightful bug' was indeed found by Tony: It was a tiny and already very dead insect of some sort!

Needless to say, while Marissa was in fact still involved with the project, she was kept well behind the scenes and was not invited to attend any further face-to-face meetings with this customer. This was much to her, and everyone's, relief, I might add.

So, what the heck is **Entomophobia**? In short, it's an excessive fear of insects, however small and harmless they may be.

5

The Molly Syndrome

Molly has worked with us for a few years. Life has not been kind to her. She was marked by her family as "the black sheep" and widowed at a young age with a newborn baby. At work, she's an average performer, easily distracted and not terribly motivated. Still, she has good intentions and simply requires reinforcement and guidance.

One would argue that weak links aren't good for business. In principle, I agree, but the human side of us must make allowances for unique circumstances. Bottom line, she should have been let go, but my conscience prevented me from allowing this every time the issue was raised. I learned to maneuver around her shortcomings and, at times, was even successful in helping bring out the best in her, tiresome though this was.

Marissa, however, showed no mercy. Her unforgiving nature fed off Molly's shortcomings like a vulture at large.

She never missed an opportunity to bluntly criticize her, and in front of other team members at that. The way she ate, the food she chose, the clothes she wore, the way she talked and laughed: anything and everything about Molly was open game for Marissa's critique.

Marissa would often storm out of her office towards Molly's cubicle and snap at her for either talking or laughing too loudly. Even though Amanda's voice, down the hall, would carry loudly when she'd get excited, the focal point of Marissa's ire was Molly alone.

Although there was little to no interaction between Marissa and Molly workwise, Marissa became obsessed with Molly's presence at the office, strategically avoiding any type of civilized communication with her.

The team would break for lunch at 12:30 or 1 pm, one group at a time. Marissa always preferred the one pm shift. A creature of habit, that was her time slot for years. However, as her irrational contempt for Molly grew, Marissa's lunchtime also became 'flexible'. She would poke her head into the area of the support team, to see if Molly was at her desk and, if she couldn't see her, would phone Tony's extension and bluntly ask: "Did she have lunch yet?" Tony knew only too well who 'she' was, but had long given up on trying to reason with Marissa.

"She—Molly, that is—is in the lunchroom. She should be back in her office shortly. Anything I can help with?"

"Just call me when she is back please."

Tony is a peaceful man who tries hard to avoid conflict. Although he couldn't comprehend this madness, he knew enough that confronting Marissa on the matter would yield no good.

In the lunchroom, while her food was warming up, Marissa would conduct a thorough inspection. If there was so much as a crumb left on the table or one of the chairs, or heaven forbid, an unwashed plate or fork in the sink, she would dash to her office, looking sternly at anyone who crossed her path.

Minutes later, an email would be received by all: "Once again there are crumbs on the table and dirty dishes in the sink. This is disgusting and completely inconsiderate of others. Please make sure to clean up your mess."

But she did not stop at that. An email addressed directly to me would immediately follow: "Please find out who left the mess and address it with them. I find it very disturbing and unpleasant to eat there. I am sure it was Molly. She is an extremely untidy person."

Yes, Molly was not particularly tidy, but nor was Amanda, Lucy or Tina. After all, it was an office, not a hospital ward. But everyone tidied their dishes before the end of a shift, and a crew of cleaners came by the office three times a week. Much ado about nothing!

One day, I was in the hallway and Marissa did not see me right away. She poked her head in, looking for Molly, and I overheard her sneering: "Is she back yet?"

Initially, I thought she might be looking for me, as earlier that morning I had stepped out of the office. "I am right here Marissa. How may I help?" Her face turned red as she murmured, "Oh, nothing, it's OK." That was odd, I thought.

I went back to my office and called Tony. "What was that all about?"

"Let me come see you. I will explain," he chuckled.

It seems her dislike for Molly had gotten so out of hand that Marissa avoided any minute in her company, especially in the lunchroom, at all cost. Every day around lunchtime, Marissa would stay in her office until she was certain Molly had already taken her break. Marissa wouldn't exit until she could clearly see that Molly was back at her desk. Still, she would phone Tony for reassurance that the 'coast was clear'.

To make matters worse, everyone was well aware of Marissa's antipathy, including Molly, although, sadly, no one talked about it. Diplomacy was certainly not a trait for which Marissa was known, even when she was 'on her best behavior'.

We were a small team and such conduct did not sit well with me. It was bullying, pure and simple.

One day, I decided to talk to Molly directly.

"What's going on between you and Marissa?"

"Oh, that. What can I say? She clearly dislikes me for whatever reason. We barely talk. She doesn't even acknowledge my existence."

"Did you have a falling out, or did anything happen to cause this?"

"Nothing that I am aware of. You know me, I get along with everyone. You know how she

is. I just let it go and try to ignore her."

"Just let it go? That doesn't seem right. Why don't you have it out with her? Ask her to meet you in the boardroom, let her explain what triggered this behaviour towards you and get to the bottom of it. Molly, no one should be treated like this. Not on my watch, in any case, and I won't put up with it. Let me help you. We must at very least try."

"Really, you think I should do that? Talk to her, that is? What if she refuses?" Molly seemed terribly uncomfortable.

"Molly, it's worth a shot. I don't like to see anyone shunned for no good reason, or for no reason at all. Go ahead, have a chat with her, calmly, and know that I have your back. Come see me afterwards."

I could see a little spark in her eyes. She would be OK.

Half an hour later Molly knocked on my door. Her face was flushed. Sporting a joyful grin, she pranced into my office and closed the door behind her.

"You wouldn't believe this. My God, I've never felt so empowered in my life. At first, she brushed me off. She was reluctant and suspicious when I asked her to meet me in the boardroom. I told her it was very important. Sorry, I had to drop your name and she finally came. I asked her straight out if I have ever done or said anything out of line to her personally to deserve this kind of attitude from her. She was taken so off guard that she was literally stammering."

"Well, did she offer an explanation?"

"No. All she said was, 'I don't know what you are talking about and I have no time for this'. I could tell she was struggling, since no one ever calls her on this stuff. But I decided this was my one and only chance and went with it."

Molly continued, "I see. You have no time, but you seem to have plenty of time to shit-talk me and criticize my every move. So, let me tell you loud and clear: I will not put up with your nastiness any longer. If you carry on attacking every move I make, I will file a formal complaint with Human Resources, and there will be plenty of examples to report, as well as a number of willing witnesses to corroborate my claims, rest assured. I will not put up with it any longer, so this ends today!"

"You will do what?! What the hell is wrong with you? I don't know what you're talking about," Marissa spluttered. "Fine, do as you please. I have no time for such nonsense."

"You don't know what I'm talking about? You call your bullying 'nonsense'? Just because I never retaliate doesn't mean that I'm ignorant of your bullying. The entire team knows. There. Your big 'secret' is out in the open."

"Are you done now? I have lots of work to finish."

"Ok then, one more thing, Marissa, that I have been itching to get off my chest for some time now. You don't scare me. I know you don't like me, and it's OK. The feeling is mutual, actually, so do us and yourself a big favour and *fuck the hell off!*

"At that point, I thought she was going to lunge at me. She looked at me with those crazy eyes. Her hands were trembling, she looked dangerously scary, and I almost lost my balance. After a moment or two, she just walked away without saying a word. My heart was racing and I was pumped. Thank you for suggesting this. I would not have done this on my own, and I feel so good. I've never told a colleague to F off, but damn it, it felt good to say it."

"A bully does not expect their victim to stand up to them," I replied. "Good for you! Hopefully this will mellow her out somewhat, although, I urge you not to hold your breath. She will stay out of your way for now, I know this much. Where is Marissa now?"

"Oh, she went back to her office, slammed the door shut and hung her 'Do not disturb' sign. Looks like one of those signs in hotels' rooms."

No one has ever threatened Marissa with a complaint to Human Resources, although a few have been tempted. I knew that it would throw her off balance, at least for a little while.

The next day Marissa called in sick. She did not make it back to the office until three days later. She never talked of the Molly incident.

Soon after, Molly resigned from her job in favour of one closer to her home. Her old clunker of a car had finally given out and she couldn't afford a new one. I was happy for her: The new job was only a short walk from her home.

The team organized a farewell outing at a restaurant and everyone was invited. Marissa, of course, boycotted the event, quite openly—but much to everyone's relief.

6

The Infamous Roll-Over

The team decided to get fit. Yeah!

For nearly a year I have been sharing stories about my wonderful personal trainer, Stacey, and how great I have been feeling since I started doing Pilates, yoga and strength training with her.

During one of our team outings, Amanda asked if my trainer would be willing to come to our office after hours and hold group sessions. The team loved the idea and committed to giving it a go. Yes, even Marissa agreed it was a good idea and the next day, everyone went shopping for mats and dumb-bells.

We were all set for our first session. Tony helped me move furniture around and we cleared a large area for everyone to set up their mats.

During the first few sessions, there was a lot of huffing, puffing and frequent 'ouches' throughout. Stacey was a great teacher. She was patient and friendly, and her incredibly fit body was inspiring, if a little intimidating. Nonetheless, she was a source of hope and motivation.

We all had a bet going to see who would drop out first. Three weeks into our workout routine, we lost Tony and Peter. Marissa stuck with it and behaved, mostly, as she had to really concentrate on the poses.

Annie was totally into it, pushing herself, while giggling at her own lack of flexibility.

Molly tends to be a gabber and Stacey occasionally had to shush her politely, saying, "Breathe, Molly. Breathe and relax."

Roland, disciplined by nature, was giving it his all. Excited to get going he had purchased a few workout outfits. He was a snazzy dresser in general and even his workout clothes were carefully matched.

Five weeks into our sessions, things were going much better for most of us. Stacey started introducing new Pilates poses that required more effort, balance and concentration.

One pose that we all struggled with at first was the roll-over. Amanda rolled over, only in the wrong direction. After a few attempts, she gave up and decided it was just too hard for her.

Annie, surprised us all by succeeding with her first attempt. We all clapped and cheered her on.

Marissa was a few minutes late that evening and was not too happy when she realized that the only vacant spot for her mat was right in front of Molly's. As the session had already started, she had no choice but to settle on that spot.

Molly was overweight, but she was a good sport and didn't let that stop her from at least trying every move. She tried the roll-over once, twice... and got it on the third attempt... and just then, with her legs stretched over her head... oops! Fucking big nasty oops.

Marissa jumped to her feet, screaming, "Oh, my God, I can't believe it! Disgusting. Really disgusting. Molly, can't you control yourself? Oh, my God, my head...you literally did it on my head. I am out of here. Shit, it stinks! Fuck!"

She continued cursing all the way to her office.

Meanwhile, Molly was completely mortified by the unfortunate incident.

"Hey, don't worry about it, shit happens," said Amanda. Poor choice of words, perhaps, but we knew she meant well.

Tony, who was still working at his desk that evening, came around to check on the commotion. I pulled him aside and briefed him, trying and failing miserably to contain my laughter.

He walked over to Molly with a big smile on his face. "Molly, you are my hero. Come on, give me a big hug," he said. "I salute you! If you had to fart, I am so glad it blew straight at Marissa."

For those of you not familiar
with the roll-over pose:

7

The Air Conditioner
Meltdown

This story may seem unbelievable to anyone who is at least somewhat endowed with reason. I kid you not, it actually happened exactly as I'm about to describe.

I was out of town meeting with a potential customer: the head of marketing of a major interior design company that I had been courting for months. Just as I turn on the PowerPoint presentation, my cell phone rings. I apologize and switch it to silent mode, which I should have done prior to the meeting. I can hear it buzzing, time after time: five missed calls, all from Marissa. I still don't answer, but the distraction is unnerving.

The meeting goes on and there is good chemistry between us; the gentleman has an excellent sense of humour, a trait that appeals to me greatly. Over the years, I've learned that injecting some humour into a serious business meeting can be helpful and productive. He seems pleased with the information presented and asks relevant questions.

I've got this. It's going well.

The phone continues to buzz, and I can see a couple of text messages too. I still don't answer.

Twenty minutes later, there's a knock on the door. The admin assistant peeks her head in, apologizes and says, "Sorry to disturb you, but Marissa has called numerous times. She didn't tell me what it's about, but I get the feeling it's urgent."

My customer must sense my distress, because he smiles and says, "No worries, go ahead and deal with it. I'll step outside for a smoke."

I call Marissa, annoyed. I've barely uttered "hello" when she starts screaming, "I have been trying to reach you, so why don't you answer? It's terrible here! Completely unbearable!"

"I am in a meeting, as you well know, and it's an important one. What's so urgent? Is someone hurt?"

"'Well, no, no one is hurt, not yet, but do you know how hot it is here today? Twenty-four degrees at the office! It's too hot (she gasps for air)! I can't concentrate! I can't do my work! The system must be broken and nobody seems to care. Can you do something? Do SOMETHING!"

I am about to erupt. Like a volcano. But I must keep my cool for the sake of my customer — and my sanity.

"Seriously? You called to report the weather? Don't you know who I'm meeting with today?" I ask, sarcastically.

"Well, the air conditioning does not work. What am I supposed to do? How can I get anything done? It is unbearable!"

I take a deep breath, totally astonished by this mad conversation.

"I am out of town, Marissa. There are 27 of you at the office. What do you expect me to do about the AC right now? Did it occur to you to contact the landlord? A technician, perhaps? Do you expect me to walk out of the meeting and jump on a flight back because you are too hot? Seriously. What the *fuck* do you expect from me?"

"Well, if you can't do anything about it, then I am going home. I can't work here today."

"Good idea," I respond. "Please go home. Take a day off if you wish."

What I really wanted to say, of course, was, "Good riddance, you little nutcracker."

I hung up and read a text sent by Tony: "So sorry, there was no stopping her! She was acting up and when I told her that a technician wouldn't be coming until tomorrow at best, she threw a fit, called me incompetent, grabbed her lunch bag and stormed out of the office. She was on a rampage and nearly walked into the wall. I am pretty sure she hurt her arm."

His text continued: "Sorry to say, but it was all rather comical. Our new hires were completely mystified, and Darla got pretty scared. Don't worry, carry on with your meeting."

The next morning, Marissa did not utter a word about her meltdown. I said, "Good morning" and she responded with what appeared to be a failed attempt at a smile. Perhaps it was just a facial spasm, or a movement gone wrong.

She stopped by the thermostat, then turned swiftly to stare at the team, but no one made eye contact with her. One brave soldier couldn't resist a chuckle. She threw a dirty look his way and stomped back to her office.

8

Are You Sure You Are Smart Enough?

Busy days at the office, multiple projects and new accounts on board: Good times!

Marissa is hard at work, meticulous to a fault, and nothing escapes her sharp eyes. She is on a mission, working long hours and sending many, many emails throughout the day. Each email is immediately followed by a phone call: "Did you see my email? When will you respond? I can't move on with the project until I get answers!"

Naturally, she dismisses any previous priorities her colleagues might have, because hers are always more pressing and far more important. When she wants answers, she harps and harps until you can't handle it anymore: You're forced to set aside whatever it is you are working on, just to provide the bloody answers and get her off your back.

As she reviews a proposal, she prepares a list of questions. Far too many questions. Most people would compose one email, perhaps two, and list all queries pertinent to the given project therein. That would make the most sense, right?

But not Marissa!

If she has 30 questions, you're sure to receive at least 30 separate emails, one after the other, within minutes of each other and with each marked 'urgent'. That is over and above her 'normal' daily correspondence, which can easily amount to 20 emails sent to each of the rest of us.

Naturally, she expects instant responses to her queries. Otherwise, she appears at your office, standing by the door and looking all frazzled and anxious. I've addressed this with her numerous times, to no avail: "That's my method, and I need to keep track of every detail," she counters. Rather than get into a futile altercation, I would review her many emails and compose one response at the end of the day, addressing all of her questions in bullet points.

As you can imagine, she did not like this one bit. It didn't go well with her moonstruck brain, and how dare I mess with her 'method'?!

The first time this happened, she stormed into my office. I was on a call and she waited, standing at the doorway, bouncing around impatiently.

As soon as I hung up, she approached my desk. She tried to put on her 'sweet face', which

can be downright freakish because you know it's an act: "Can I ask you to provide answers by responding to each email please? I find it very confusing to have all the answers in one document!"

"Sorry," I answered calmly, "but that would conflict with my method."

Her forced smile turned into a frown. 'That's more like it', I thought. She knew enough not to push me further and stormed out of my office.

Delegating work does not come easily to Marissa. She trusts no one. However, these are unusually busy times: the workload is far too heavy and the timelines, ambitious. Even our 'superhero' feels the pressure.

She comes to see me, and explains all that she has to do, exasperated. Sweat beads form across her face, and her chin quivers as she talks. I know what's coming next and don't want to pass up this rare occasion. 'Let her say it,' I think — admittedly, with some glee — to myself. She struggles even to utter the words. It's clearly a breaking point for Marissa, who is about to ask for help!

I suggest she ask Amanda for assistance. "Are you sure?" she bawls out, as her dubious eyes widen.

I have witnessed such reactions many a time, I find it disturbingly comical by now. "Well, you need help and she is available. Go ahead, give it a shot," I respond.

Amanda is a lovely, kind lady. She is liked by everyone and has been with us for many years. She is definitely capable, although, at times, self-doubting. I give her a quick courtesy heads-up so that she can prepare herself for the whirlwind that's about to bolt into her office.

Amanda gets anxious easily and when she does, her face and neck break out in hives. She gets flustered and out of breath. I can hear the quiver in her voice and try to assure her that it's a rather simple task, not to worry.

Marissa marches to Amanda's office, stands next to her, and looks directly at her with piercing eyes. Marissa lowers her head, forcing Amanda to maintain direct eye contact, and utters in a stern voice: "I was told you are available to help with a project!"

Amanda's eyes are wide open, panic-stricken. "Yes, I guess so. What do you need me to do?" she asks, as she repeatedly brushes the same long stands of hair off her face, a nervous tic for which she is known.

"OK, listen carefully, I don't have time to waste, so look at me and listen!" Marissa demands.

"I'm listening, I'm listening," Amanda answers anxiously.

Marissa explains in great detail the information that is required on the spreadsheet. Now and then she pauses, looks at Amanda, trying to detect if she is 'getting it'.

Amanda just nods her head up and down, continuously, like a bobble-head. It's as if she has lost all muscle control. Poor girl. She finally manages to say, "I understand."

"Are you sure?" Marissa asks, continuing, **"Are you sure you are smart enough to handle this?"**

Totally bewildered by this point, Amanda's face is bright

red, her hands shake and her palms are sweaty. "I think so. It doesn't seem complicated," she murmurs. (Let's take a moment to clarify an important point: That spreadsheet project involved basic data entry—no fancy formulas or calculations, but simply data copied from several documents over to one).

"OK, do just a few entries and let me check it. There's no time to waste. You must get it right."

She walks towards the door, then stops abruptly. Turning her head, she stares straight at Amanda. With her pudgy index finger wagging, Marissa again asks, "You are sure you can handle this, right?" She does not wait for an answer and waddles angrily back to her office, convinced it won't be done properly and most likely already rehearsing her 'I told you so' speech.

Later that day, Amanda comes to see me, all worn out, as could be expected.

I try to calm her down, offering her a glass of water as she describes in great detail the unnerving event, mimicking Marissa's piercing crazy eyes and wagging index finger. We have a good laugh and reckon that this is certainly a story to be remembered and recounted. Yet another one for the books.

Well, the project was completed, on time and error-free, undoubtedly out of sheer fear!

Marissa of course, fully expecting Amanda to fail, looked simultaneously bemused and defeated.

Imagine asking for help and bluntly saying to your would-be helper, **"Are you sure you're smart enough?!"**

9

Bad Habits

Amanda and I are casual smokers. On days I was at the office, I would pass by her cubicle holding a cigarette and she would respond, enthusiastically, "Yes, let's go. I could use one right now."

When Marissa found out about my smoking, she was understandably stunned. You see, I had been smoke-free for well over 20 years. So, what happened? Life happened. It has a way of creeping up on us, altering our plans and messing up our priorities. And, at times, it takes us to places we'd rather avoid. But such is life. Since this story really isn't about me, let's just leave it at that for now, cool?

On a number of occasions, as Amanda and I stood outside smoking away, Marissa would walk past us, on her way in or out of the office, barely saying hello. Instead, she would give us a harsh, long, scornful look. Most times we just laughed it off. It is Marissa after all: always disapproving, always feeling superior to everyone else, and seldom passing up an opportunity to speak her mind in the most unforgiving manner.

We were well past the stage of caring or taking it personally, which, no doubt, irritated her greatly. She had long since given up on any attempt to bully me: While her mouth shoots arrows, my daggers, she has found out, can be just as sharp, if not sharper. Amanda, however, was still easy prey for Marissa, although not in my company, where she felt protected.

On days that I was out of the office, travelling or otherwise, Amanda would smoke at the back of the building, in the parking lot, hiding between cars — ideally large vans if she could find them — just to avoid a potential encounter with Marissa.

So many times, she wanted to tell Marissa to mind her own business, but as soon as Amanda would catch a glimpse of those beady, crazy eyes, she would freeze and wouldn't be able to utter a word.

There is never a good time to pick a fight, but it is fundamentally wrong to do so on a Friday, what with the weekend just hours away.

But Marissa operates by her own set of rules.

Amanda and I had just completed a long and tedious project after working from early morning, through lunch. At around 4 pm she came by my office holding a cigarette. I didn't give her a chance to ask, but immediately grabbed my pack and off we went. We were both tired, but pleased that neither of us would have to work through the weekend.

We stood in the designated smoking zone. It was a beautiful, warm and sunny day, and the weekend forecast looked promising. We talked about our plans, both excited to enjoy a well-deserved break.

Sadly, it was a short-lived break, as Marissa soon popped out of nowhere. We didn't see her

coming. If we had, we would have walked towards the back of the building.

She stood there, her glasses resting on the tip of her nose, face all red as she bellowed, "That's a disgusting habit. Shame on you both. Do you not realize the damage you are doing to your body? Really disgusting!"

She was right, of course, however...

I took a puff, exhaled slowly and replied calmly:

"Thank you for your sincere concern. Yes, a bad habit indeed, but we all have them, wouldn't you agree, Marissa? Have you given any thought as to how you are going to manage yours?"

Her eyes widened, and her head jutted forward as she hollered, "What are you talking about?"

"Oh, Marissa, surely you know a bad habit when you see one."

"What bad habit? What are you on about?" she shrieked. Of course, in her own world, she is one of nature's rare and perfect creations.

"Come on, Marissa, are you seriously asking me to state the obvious?" I sized her up,

taking in her plump, short figure from top to bottom.

Marissa, with her nostrils twitching, was speechless for once. She stood still for a few seconds, desperately searching for a comeback and looking terribly flustered. She had nothing! She gasped, turned away and waddled towards her car, still shaking her head from side to side.

10

You Said
She Was Stupid?!

Marissa, with her many quirks, is still a very competent employee. That being said, with Marissa, even good things are somehow entangled with madness.

Product prototypes are always required before we go into manufacturing. If we're lucky, the first one is a go, but statistically, we almost always require a second or third before approval. More often than not, the obstacle is Marissa!

A long-awaited prototype has finally arrived. The factory was three weeks behind schedule, and, to make matters worse, it was held up by Customs as well. Once the item was at our office, the team was summoned to the boardroom. Everyone shared a sense of urgency.

We put the prototype to the test. I could sense the tension in the air, and then I saw the disappointed and questioning faces. Something wasn't right. It looked so much better on paper. Those fearful of Marissa do not dare voice their opinion, so I have to break the ice.

"The overall look is good, but the fit is off and this compromises the integrity of the design. It needs adjustments. What do you think, everyone?"

At this point, the team spoke up, one after the other, offering productive feedback, and, yes, there were a few discussions happening at once—something I know throws Marissa off balance.

She stands in front of the prototype, looking disapproving, sweat beads forming on her upper lip. "There is nothing wrong with this and you don't know what you are talking about," she says. "We need to get the vendor in here. Only they will understand."

"Team," I said, "Your feedback is right on, but I agree, we need to have the vendor here so they can see and hear directly from us. We'll arrange a meeting for tomorrow morning."

As you can imagine, Marissa was not happy, but knew she had no choice. The team had spoken.

The next morning two of the vendor's representatives were at our office. I didn't see them entering the building, but it seems Marissa was waiting for them outside so she could hurry them to the boardroom before the rest of us joined—a practice only too well known to us all.

By the time Roland and I arrived at the boardroom, the vendor had been given Marissa's version of events.

"Oh, hello," one of the reps said. "It's nice to see you two. Look, I just want to say that we measured and inspected the prototype carefully before shipping it to you. You have to believe us; we knew it was urgent and we did all that we could."

"Mr. Sutton, we appreciate that you took the time to be here today, and we do not question your integrity. There are, however, a few concerns we need to address, and an additional prototype will be required. We cannot approve this one as is."

"But we can fix it at manufacturing. I am sure these are minor details."

"Mr. Sutton, with all due respect, that won't be happening. We can't possibly take such a risk."

We pointed out the spec deviations and Mr. Sutton actually agreed with us. "I would like to bring Annie in," I said. "She understands the technical spec inside out and would be able to pinpoint what changes are required."

"Annie," screeched Marissa, "What do we need her for?"

"Marissa, you know very well that Annie can help and has helped us on numerous occasions. We don't have the luxury of time. I am bringing her in."

Sadly, anyone who does not openly fear Marissa gains her suspicion by default. Such was the case with Annie.

Annie, a veteran employee who is respected and liked by all, was our unofficial technical expert. She did not hold a title *per se*, but her assessments carried weight. I would often seek her advice on a prototype, and in most instances, apply her words of wisdom to action. She never let me down.

Annie, an immigrant from Spain, had yet to master English, but knew enough to get by. Her work was meticulous and professional.

Just as Annie walked into the boardroom, my phone rang. It was an important call I had to take. "Annie, my dear, please review this and offer your comments. I will be in my office. Please come see me when you are done."

She nodded with a smile.

About 30 minutes later, Annie came to see me. She was observant, always knowing exactly what goes on around the office. A timid lady with exceptional manners, she never spoke ill of anyone. This time, however, she had a story to tell...

It seems she went into great analytical detail and the vendor agreed with her. Her input, to them, was invaluable.

As Annie made her way out of the boardroom, the vendor, who always conversed with Annie in French and assumed she spoke no English, was overheard saying to Marissa:

"I don't understand, Marissa. You said she was stupid, but she is not stupid at all. She really understands this stuff and I'm glad she was here to help."

Marissa tried to alert him that Annie was within earshot, but it was too late.

Annie turned her head slightly, enough to notice Marissa's face burning red.

"I'm happy to help, Mr. Sutton," Annie said in French with a smile, then added in English: "Have a lovely day, Mr. Sutton. See you next time."

I have known Mr. Sutton for a long time. He never spoke of that incident with me. He was far too embarrassed. However, he did make a point of complimenting Annie's expertise whenever the opportunity presented itself.

11

The Christmas Lunch

For a few years in a row, our team shared a nice tradition: On the last day of work, just before the Christmas shutdown, we had a communal lunch, with every dish representing the cultural background of an individual on the team. Ours was a diverse group. We enjoyed delicacies from Italy, Greece, Spain, Eastern Europe, Asia and the Middle East, with only one rule: bring your favourite dish.

We sat at a long table in the front room, bright with natural daylight, and our creative and talented Annie was in charge of decorating the tree. The atmosphere was always joyful and festive.

The first three years of this tradition were missed by Marissa as she was on vacation, much to everyone's relief.

But on the fourth year, there was no escape: she stayed in town for the holidays and immediately took charge of the lunch project. She fired a long email off to everyone, asking us to complete a survey. She needed to know well in advance what each of us would be bringing to ensure the menu was 'well-balanced', she explained.

Part of the fun was the surprise element of each dish and letting employees tell the story behind their traditional holiday favourite. Some of the recipes had been passed on for many generations. Of course, not everyone likes to, or can, cook, and that was perfectly OK: They could purchase a ready-made dish, dessert or drinks. The idea was primarily about all of us having lunch together, as on typical workdays our busy team members ate in shifts.

After a few days of Marissa badgering us with reminders, the somewhat fearful employees completed the list and were relieved to get her off their backs — or so they thought.

The next morning, I was at the office early. As employees started coming in and settling at their desks, I could hear grumbling, cursing and laughing. Naturally, I was curious, so I walked over to chat.

"Good morning, did you see the love letter we all got?" one of my colleagues asked.

"Good morning, team, and no I have not. But let me take a wild guess: Marissa?"

Josh handed me his copy. "Don't worry, we aren't upset. This is just far too funny."

It was hardly a love letter, but once you considered the source, all rules were out. Here is an excerpt of the list Marissa had them fill, along with her 'insightful' thoughts:

Name	Dish	Comments
Julia	Mohammara (Middle Eastern dish with lamb)	Lamb? Really, does anyone eat lamb?
Natasha	Pirozhki (Russian stuffed buns)	There is too much starch already, can you bring something else?
Tony	Portuguese chicken with roasted potatoes	Don't mix the chicken with the potatoes, keep them apart at all times
Josh	Party sandwiches platter from Olga's	These are disgusting, what else can you bring?
Josh	Panettone fruit cake	I hope it's not from Mama Mia, they don't put enough fruit in

I read through the notes and my initial reaction was a mouthful of 'What the fuck', but then again, it's Marissa! I just burst out laughing. What a bloody party pooper, I thought.

You have to understand, food was critically important to Marissa. She never took it lightly and did not trust most grocery stores, let alone food cooked by other people.

"OK, team, let's put this in perspective; no matter what you end up bringing, it will be subject to merciless critique, so just stick to your original plan and bring any dish you feel like sharing. I will handle the nutcracker."

Marissa came into the office around 10 am that morning. After a few minutes at her office and a chance to check her emails, she came to see me.

"Good morning," she said forcing an off-balance smile. "I forgot to copy you on an email I sent to the team, you know, about our lunch in a couple of weeks."

"Yes, the lunch," I tried to keep a straight face. "I actually saw the list."

"Oh, you did? And, what do you think? Wasn't I right about some of their choices?"

"I seriously doubt you want to hear what I really think, Marissa. Let's just say, the menu remains as is."

"What do you mean?" she whined. "Then there will be nothing for me to eat. Did you see what some of them plan to bring? Don't you think it's disgusting? Who needs all that starch?

All the girls are getting fat as it is!"

I could not believe she just said that!

"Well, then, Marissa, how about you bring your own lunch and just eat with us. As for the starch, I didn't know you are watching your diet: not with that oversized bag of cookies on your desk."

"These are healthy cookies with little sugar!" she snapped.

"I am sure they are delicious. That is probably why they come in a family-sized bag. Look, Marissa, this lunch tradition has been going on for a few years and everyone enjoys it, so please, lighten up. Let's not turn it into an unpleasant ordeal, not before Christmas."

She got up, gave me a deep and penetrating gaze, and stormed out of my office.

Coincidently, she did join us for the lunch, and, while she boycotted a couple of the dishes, she displayed a very healthy appetite indeed.

12

Bloody Meat Pies

Monday mornings are typically a least favoured time of the week, especially when you have to hustle through slow-moving traffic during a miserable January snowstorm.

After nearly an hour on the road, for a trip that usually took no more than 10 minutes, I made it to the office, stressed and annoyed. I had five minutes to get out of my coat and boots, grab a coffee and hop on a conference call. Not a great way to start the day, not to mention the week.

My to-do list seemed to be getting longer as the morning progressed: numerous emails to read, voice messages to respond to and a big report due by day's end. As soon as the conference call ended, I took a deep breath and said to myself, "OK, buckle up and get on with it." The thought, however, was interrupted by the whirlwind that is Marissa. As she stormed in, I thought, 'Fuck! Not her, not now, not today!'

"I must talk to you. I know you are busy, but it cannot wait."

"I'm extremely busy, Marissa. What is so urgent?"

She pulled a chair out. Oh no, I thought to myself, this was hardly going to be a brief one.

"I need you to talk to Molly. She won't listen to me and I can't take that smell. I can't work like this. I can smell it all over the office."

"The smell? OK, let's have it. I hate to ask, but I feel I have to, so — what smell, Marissa?"

"Well, you know I hate fish. I hate the smell. It really gets to me."

"Yes, I know you don't care for fish. How does this have anything to do with Molly?"

"Well, for a few days now, all she eats for lunch are tuna salads. The smell is disgusting. It lingers through the day and makes me nauseous. I even smell it on my clothes when I go home. I have to dry clean everything. It's not right and you must talk to her."

She was ranting and talking so quickly that I thought she was having a breakdown in front of me. Shit, she is mad, bloody mad, so how can I possibly reason with her?

I looked at the time and realized I was falling behind.

"OK, let me see what I can do."

"So, you'll talk to her? You'll tell her to stop bringing that smelly fish to the office?"

"I will talk to her. Now please, I have lots to do."

When she shut the door behind her, I held my head between my hands and laughed uncontrollably.

Towards the end of the day, I asked Molly to see me. I had been travelling extensively for four weeks and this was my first day in the office in a while. As Molly walked in, I noticed a change in her.

"Hey, you, you are looking good. What have you been up to?" I asked.

"Oh, you noticed," she seemed pleased. "Well, I didn't tell the team because I didn't want to disappoint them should I fail. I started a diet five weeks ago and, so far, I've lost 16 pounds. I still have a way to go, but I feel good."

"Good for you, Molly. It certainly shows. I'm proud of you and promise I won't say a word. What type of diet are you following?"

"It's simple, really. I pretty much eat the same meals every day for a week, then I change the menu the following week. For example, this past week was fruit for breakfast, a big tuna salad for lunch and vegetable soup for dinner."

"That certainly sounds healthy and congrats on losing all these pounds. Did you say that this past week was tuna for lunch? So, what's on next week's menu?"

I started the diet on a Tuesday, so I count the week from Tuesday to the following Monday. Although I adore tuna, tomorrow is a new menu, so probably chicken for a week."

"OK, Molly, I have to come clean. This is actually pretty fucking hilarious."

I told her about my earlier chat with Marissa.

Fortunately, Molly has a great sense of humour and found the whole thing amusing too.

We agreed that, since 'tuna week' ended today, we will just let Marissa believe that she's won. There will be no tuna, at least not for a couple of weeks.

The next day, around lunchtime, I got a whiff of a nasty odour. It was something unfamiliar and rather awful. I prepared myself, thinking Marissa would come storming in again. I waited and waited, but no, no Marissa. I had been spared.

Wednesday lunchtime comes and fuck, it's that smell again. What the hell is it? I braced myself, expecting Marissa to appear at my office door, but again, no: no Marissa.

Thursday lunchtime: Oh, for God's sake, not that smell again!

I call Tony and ask him to see me.

He shows up within seconds, fingers pinching his nose. "Oh, you can smell it all the way to your office. Lucky you," he chuckles.

"Tony, what is it that smell? This is the third day now. What's going on?"

"What do you think? Come on, I challenge you to guess."

"Marissa! What has she done now?"

"She discovered these meat pies. She bakes them for about an hour and by the time we all go for lunch, the kitchen reeks. We told her the smell is strong, but she didn't care.

She just sits there devouring them, two in a sitting. So today, we just waited for her to finish and went for our lunch later. Julia has been spraying perfume all day to kill the smell. What can we do? You know how Marissa is. She'll bite my head off if I dare comment. The problem is, she bought a large box of those pies and keeps it in the freezer. I'm afraid we're going to have to put up with it for a while."

"Thank you, Tony. Let me see what I can do. Honestly, the smell is pretty foul."

Some days, I felt like I was running a circus rather than a business.

"Marissa, would you please come see me?"

She sat down, looking pretty content following her meal.

"So, have you noticed that Molly no longer brings tuna salads for lunch?"

"Yes, thank you very much. What a relief. I hope she was not upset?"

Yeah, right, because Marissa was so deeply concerned for Molly.

"She was not upset. Now, let's talk about your choice of lunch for the last three days. Have you been enjoying your meat pies?"

"How did you know I am eating meat pies? Did you see them in the freezer? They are so good. You should try one."

I have yet to meet anyone who gets equally as excited over food. It's actually a little disturbing.

"Oh, I did not have to see them, Marissa. They communicated with me loud and clear by transmitting a very powerful, almost deadly scent."

"What? What do you mean?"

"I am surprised, Marissa. I thought your sense of smell was super sensitive, what with the tuna issue and all. Did you eat with the team today?"

"No, actually, they said they were busy. I was alone in the lunchroom."

"I see, so it never occurred to you that perhaps that room-clearing scent is what kept them away?"

"What scent, the tuna?"

"No, no Marissa, not the tuna. No one seems to mind the tuna but you. I am talking about your meat pies and the intense odour they omit."

"They do?! I didn't notice. Oh my, what shall I do? Should I not eat them here anymore? Wow, that would be too bad. I really enjoy them." She gave me a hopeful look, desperately seeking empathy.

"Eat what you want, meat pies and all, but the next time Molly brings a tuna salad, or anything else for that matter, just put up with it, please. And, most importantly, keep me out of these ridiculous discussions!"

She got up very slowly, her lips trembling and eyes widened with fury — powerless fury. She was not happy.

13

Marissa's Secret Crush

The lease on our building was up and we decided to move to a new location rather than renew. We have had issues with maintenance and the timing was perfect.

Our head office brought in our company's preferred corporate real estate agent, Patrick White, to conduct a search on our behalf.

I gathered the team to announce the decision and asked everyone to send me a list of must-have features in our would-be new location. Marissa was the first to respond with a long wish list of points, some of which were valid, but others that were typical 'Marissa ideas' which I, naturally, dismissed.

After a few back and forth calls with Patrick, he had a clear idea of the location and type of office we desired. After confirming the first eight appointments, Patrick booked his trip.

Marissa somehow found out about the upcoming visit and showed up at my office in an unusually good mood. She was giddy. I never dreamt I would have the occasion to use this word to describe Marissa, but giddy she was indeed.

"Hi! I hear corporate is sending a real estate agent next week," she said.

"That's right. It will be a busy two weeks, but we have some promising prospects."

"Who are they sending?"

"A guy by the name of Patrick White. I've heard of him, but never met him in person. Why do you ask?"

"Oh, they are sending Patrick." She sighed with a big smile. "I met him once and he is really nice."

"Good to know. I'll be spending two weeks with him visiting various places."

She was still smiling as if her expression was frozen in pause mode. Strange. I had never seen her react like that before. Visits from head office always caused her some distress, so I wondered what was up.

Marissa has been living with a guy for a number of years: a desperate soul, or perhaps just a very brave soldier. I was actually quite fond of him. He was always pleasant to talk to.

Two weeks later.

I grabbed my purse and headed to the door to pick Patrick up at the airport. Just as I opened the door, Marissa came running. Her hair was freshly done and she was wearing a dress! She even had on high heels, which she'd given up years ago after a knee injury. Weird.

"Are you going to the airport? Perhaps I can go with you and we can take Patrick for lunch."

"That's a nice thought, Marissa, but I've ordered lunch already and it should arrive within the hour. We were planning on working, but another time, maybe."

Her smile turned into an obviously disappointed frown. She was acting strangely and I got a disturbing vibe.

"Got to go, his flight has just landed!"

At the airport, Patrick spotted me and walked over with a smile. We had connected on LinkedIn to at least get an idea of what the other looked like. He was handsome and pleasant, and the latter was comforting since we would be spending two intense weeks together. We had a friendly chat on our drive to the office.

We arrived at the office and there was Marissa at the door, right where I'd left her.

"Hi Patrick, so nice to see you again!" she said in an unusually high-pitched voice, swiftly followed by a laugh gone wrong. She actually snorted!

"Oh, hello, Larissa, nice to see you too." She stood there smiling, not even bothering to correct him.

I showed Patrick to our guest office to settle his laptop and files and told him I would be back shortly.

"Hey, Tony, can you please come by my office?"

"Right away," he said, enthusiastic as ever. He came to

my office door and said, "I have a feeling you want to talk about Marissa, or should I say, Larissa? I know. We have all been wondering about her. She's been acting very strangely these past few days and especially today, pacing the hallway back and forth since you left for the airport. She is wearing a dress! She never wears dresses to work!"

"Well, Tony, my guess is as good as yours. She is acting like a woman possessed."

We didn't get a chance to wrap up, since Marissa came barging in, clearly struggling in her high heels.

"Are you taking Patrick out to dinner tonight? I am sure he wants to see the city. I can recommend a nice restaurant downtown. I can join you! I can drive!"

Things were getting spooky. Marissa was rarely enthusiastic about visits from head office. I had to wonder what the hell she was up to.

"Tony, would you mind giving us a moment please?"

He winked at me and closed the door to my office as he stepped out.

"Are you OK, Marissa? You seem rather anxious."

"Of course, I am OK. Why wouldn't I be? Why, did anyone say anything? What did you hear and why are they talking about me?" Her words blurted out so fast that she was totally out of breath.

"Calm down, Marissa, this is not an interrogation. You've seemed on edge ever since you heard of Patrick's visit. Is there anything you'd like to talk about?"

As soon as I mentioned Patrick's name, her face relaxed and her eyes got all dreamy.

"Oh, my God, Marissa, you like Patrick. Like really, *really* like Patrick. You do know he is married and has four kids, not to mention he is some 15 years your junior, right?"

"You are crazy. What are you talking about?" Her face turned red, her lips quivered and her eyes twitched.

"It's OK, Marissa, I get it. He is very handsome and sweet. I hardly blame you. Don't worry. Let this be our little secret? I promise, I won't tell."

"Oh, my God, this is so embarrassing. Was I that obvious? I barely know him. I met him once and he was so nice. Please, please, please, don't tell anyone. You know I love Roger and this is crazy. Did anyone say anything? What are they saying?"

"Nothing at all, other than you look nice in a dress."

"Oh, phew!"

Little white lies to the rescue.

14

The President's Grand Visit

Our office had relocated to a new building. It was a big undertaking, but everyone was excited. The new place was modern, sun-filled and spacious. It was good for morale and productivity. Everyone was eager to find out which office or cubicle would be theirs.

One of the offices was particularly large and although I could have made it my own, I settled on a smaller one, which offered more privacy. As for the big office, I was pretty sure who would claim it as their own: Marissa!

As I have already told you, Marissa has kept every document ever sent to her over the last 12 years. She prints every email, regardless of the level of importance, then files it away. Over the years, she kept on adding filing cabinets to her office. When she ran out of floor space, she asked for stackable units. Once these additional cabinets were full, we had to clear the stock room and add more for her there.

Eventually, we ran out of space altogether, so she converted her large desk into an open space filing unit. Walking past her office you can barely see her short figure, nestled amidst the piles and piles of paper. Somehow this madness worked for her.

Once we were all settled in the new building, we decided to host a cocktail reception. It was a great opportunity to mingle with our customers and colleagues, not to mention a few special guests from our head office in Europe. Even our president was to attend, which was quite an honour!

The team was great, with each member accepting a task, from coordinating food, drinks and decorations to planning the entertainment. We bought some new plants and decorated the walls with interesting artwork and team photos. All was ready, or so we thought.

Marissa, who did not participate in the planning process, was strangely quiet for a few days... until she suddenly shifted into panic mode.

She barged into my office, dragging poor Tony along.

"Oh, my God, our president is coming, all these VPs, our major customers... What am I going to do?"

"What do you mean? In case you haven't noticed, the team has worked tirelessly to get everything done. What exactly is your concern?"

"Well, my office. I can't let them see my office. What am I going to do? Where can I store all the files on my desk, all the samples, the racks? I need boxes. I need some help.

The party is only two days away and I have so much work to do."

The outside wall of her office is glass from top to bottom. Even if the door were to remain closed during the event, you'd have to be blind or totally drunk not to notice the bizarre set up in there.

I looked over at Tony, who was trying hard to wipe away a devilish smile. "Any ideas in mind, Tony?" I asked.

"Not really. The stock room is packed, the spare room already has some 20 boxes she moved there last month and, short of shipping it all to her house, I can't create more space here."

"To my house? Are you insane? Do you know how many boxes there are?"

"Well, Marissa, it seems you will just have to hope no one walks into your office," I said.

"I can't do that! What will the president think of me? What about the customers? I can't let them see my office, so can someone help me?"

She looked at Tony, exasperated.

"All I can do at this short notice is get you some boxes. You can at least pack away all the piles on your desk if you think it would make a difference. You will have to charge some to your cost centre, since the office budget is already maxed."

I could tell Tony had just about had it, and I didn't blame him. Marissa never offered any help with the party and kept a very low profile while everyone was busy with preparations.

"Can we ask the company next door if we can store some boxes for a couple of days? Do you know any one there?" asked Marissa.

Wow, she was really desperate.

Tony was a very friendly guy who was at ease around others. He had already befriended some of the guys next door. He went over, gave them a heads up on our very unusual request and,

with a perfect twist of his humour, they agreed to store her boxes for two days.

Marissa was under tremendous pressure. She dashed to her car and drove to the nearest office supplies store, buying as many boxes as she could fit in her small car. She packed for hours. According to the alarm system register, she logged out of the building just before midnight.

The next day, there were well over 30 large boxes stacked outside her office. She clearly hoped someone would come to her rescue and help her move them next door. Her beautiful desk was fully seen for the first time by many of our colleagues.

Tony was loving every moment. He popped in to see me, laughing his heart out.

"You know me. I will help her, but not yet. Let me have some fun with this first. She is sweating and cursing. I shouldn't laugh, but boy, she'd had this coming."

The boxes were moved eventually, with Tony's help, of course. The day after the party, Tony left the red trolley outside Marissa's office and said to her, "You can bring the boxes back one by one. They are working late tonight, next door, so you have plenty of time."

Poor Marissa. Huffing and puffing, her body still aching from all the packing, she waddled back and forth down the sidewalk, pushing a red trolley with irritating squeaky wheals. A few of us approached the window to watch this rather unique and entertaining spectacle.

15

Righteous Marissa

The company next door to our new office held a major end-of-season sale of their lucrative outerwear line. These items, both for children and adults, were highly popular at retail stores around the world. The garments were also costly, making a 70% discount sale an attractive one indeed.

The first day was open to employees only, while the following five days were for family and friends. Around 100 guests came each evening and employees and guests were required to bring along non-perishable food items, all of which were donated to a local food bank before Christmas.

In no time, our happy-go-lucky Tony had befriended a few of the employees next door, which earned us all an invitation to the big sale's opening day—and the option for each one of us to invite up to four guests.

The second year of the big sale, we had an intern named Nathalie working for us part time. She was a young single mother who was also working hard to complete her marketing degree while raising a young boy. I was impressed by her drive and determination, and I naturally wanted to help her out if I could.

The big sale was only two days away. We were all set to go together at closing time, around 5:30 pm. The sale was set to open as of 3 pm. Nathalie asked me if it would be possible for her to attend the sale at 3:30 pm, so that she could make it on time to pick up her son at kindergarten. I agreed, of course.

The next day, I barely had a chance to remove my boots when Marissa came storming into my office, slamming the door as she entered.

"We have to talk!" she said in a stern voice.

"Sure, come in, make yourself comfortable," I said with full-on sarcasm.

"Did you know that the new girl is planning to attend the sale at 3:30 instead of at 5:30

like the rest of us?"

"The new girl has name, and a pretty one too. Now, what exactly is your issue? I told Nathalie it was OK for her to attend at 3:30, seeing her shift ends at 3 pm anyway."

"Well, that's not fair. Why should she get a first crack at everything? Why can't she go at 5:30 like the rest of us?"

I took a deep breath, collected myself and supressed the urge to pour my jug of water on her head.

"Nathalie, as you know, is juggling school, work and a

little boy all on her own. Certain situations require flexibility
and I, for one, am more than willing to accommodate her.
Besides, she is 5'10" and a perfect size four, hardly the di-
mensions you'd be shopping for. There are hundreds of
items for sale, so what exactly is your concern?"

She got up slowly, her lips quivering. She saw the fire
in my eyes and knew me well enough to realize she had
pushed just a little too far.

So, did she drop the subject? Hell, no!

Unbeknown to me, she ranted about this to every team
member, ensuring that news of the 'unjust' issue would make
its way to Nathalie eventually.

The day of the sale, I noticed Nathalie was still at her
desk although it was 4:30 pm.

"Hey Nathalie, what's up? Did you make it next door
already?"

"I've asked the babysitter to pick up Sam at the nursery.
It's OK. I will go at 5:30 with everyone. I don't want to
cause any issues, but thank you anyways."

Fuck. Marissa!

Tony saw me chatting with Nathalie and followed me
to my office.

"I'm really sorry. We all told Marissa that we really didn't
mind Nathalie going early. Most of us are parents and we
understand, but she was going on and on, driving us all
crazy. Poor Nathalie got so scared; I think she made other
arrangements."

The following year, I had to go on a business trip during the big sale and Tony was left in charge.

Upon my return, he came by my office, shaking his head from side to side.

"You'd better sit down for this and let me close the door. I would rather you hear this from me. Here, I brought you some coffee. I wish I had whiskey to pour in it, but we have a no alcohol policy at the office, right?" He winked and smiled, trying to downplay the news he was about to share.

He recounted the events, trying desperately to inject humour into his tale, for fear of my reaction, perhaps.

"She did what?! Are you serious? I can't believe the bloody hypocrisy!" I said, promptly calling Marissa to come to my office for a talk.

"What, now?" she asked.

"Yes, now!"

She walked in, taking small hesitant steps, and took a seat next to Tony. She did not utter a word.

"So, Marissa, good finds at the sale for you this year?"

She seemed confused, unsure of where I was going with this.

"OK, let's cut the crap! Last year, you made a bloody fuss over our intern attending the sale a couple of hours early, for fear that she might purchase the lot and leave nothing for you. You made such an issue scaring the poor girl, who was then forced to pay for a babysitter out of her small income. What were your exact words? Oh yes, 'unjust and unfair'! Yet, you didn't hesitate for a second, I've heard, to sneak your neighbour in through the side door, bypassing a line of some 120 guests who had been waiting patiently for nearly two hours?!"

A dreadful sound of silence filled the office.

She was not making eye contact. Staring at the floor, she murmured, "My neighbour just found out she is pregnant. It's hard for her to stand for a long time, and, well, there was a big line up."

"I see. So, you thought it was OK to sneak her in ahead of all the other guests, some of whom had showed up an hour early hoping to make it to the front of the line?"

"Well, yes, but she is six weeks pregnant."

"Did you coordinate with Tony ahead of time, or just assume no one would notice?

Actually, don't

bother answering. That's not really a question. But this one is: Remember Nathalie? Does the name ring a bell, *Ms. Justice*?!"

16

Guardian of the Samples

Our largest customer tasked us with a complete do-over of their product line. It was a major project that would take around 12 months to complete, but the creative team was enthusiastic and on board.

Marissa was appointed to work with the creative team. Her role was to ensure all samples met the specifications, were on time and were visually appealing. This was a sound business decision: despite her quirks, Marissa was meticulous to a fault. She always paid attention to the easy-to-miss details. Her talents, however — as we know — always came with a price.

The team met every morning to discuss their progress, challenges and risk mitigation. A full hour was allocated to these meetings, but they often went over time since Marissa came equipped with a laundry list of critiques. As soon as innocent team members would move on to the next topic, they were met with a terse holler: "I am not done!"

It took an awful lot of patience and tongue-biting to get through these meetings with Marissa. Occasionally I would take the team out for drinks after, either to a bar or my home, so they could release steam. These outings were filled with laughter, uncensored tongue-lashings and raw cursing. Therapy at its best!

Three weeks before our final presentation, most of the samples were in. Nonetheless, Marissa switched into panic mode. She drove us all mad with emails, phone calls and ambushed 'meetings' in the hallway and parking lot. (A former employee once told me that we must develop a Marissa survival guide and hand it to all team members...).

Marissa, ever the control freak, set up the boardroom with racks and shelves so she could keep track of the samples. The boardroom was at the front of the building and she could not see it from her office. This, by itself, drove her crazy. She would get up frequently and walk over, just to ensure no one was 'messing' things up.

She hung a sign on the boardroom door that read, "PLEASE **DON'T** TOUCH THE SAMPLES!"

Then, just to make sure she got her message across, she sent an email to everyone that read, "**Important**: The samples are in a particular order. Please don't touch or move them. If you need to look at them, let me know and I will go with you."

If you think that these samples were classified top secret data...you are wrong. Very wrong.

A few days before the presentation, poor, unsuspecting Roland was in the boardroom taking pictures of the samples, at my request, when he was startled by a frantic Marissa.

"What are you doing here? Don't move my samples! Don't touch this! Are your hands clean? Why didn't you tell me you'd be in here? Didn't you get my email?"

Startled by Marissa's mania, Roland leapt back, dropping his camera and banging his knee on the metal rack. Desperately trying to catch the camera before it hit the ground, he ended up face down on the floor himself.

"What the fuck? Are you mad, woman? Why do you have to sneak up like this? What the hell is wrong with you?"

Marissa then realized that he might be hurt and tried to help him get up, only she lost her balance and fell flat on her ass as well. Feeling rather embarrassed and in some discomfort, she tried to pull herself up, to no avail.

Roland, already hurt, did not want to risk a back injury trying to lift her off the ground. Mostly, however, he was a strong believer in Karma and took some pleasure in seeing Marissa flat on her ass. He inched over to the phone and called Tony: "Hey, man, we need your help in the boardroom. Get Peter to come along, please, 'cause this is a two-person job."

Marissa's face was bright red. She hated feeling helpless and worse yet was the possibility of being found in such a compromising position. She knew the team would crack endless jokes about it.

Tony walked by my office and motioned for me to join him. "Trouble in the boardroom," he said.

"Oh, let me take a wild guess," I replied. "Marissa?"

Peter, from maintenance, joined us as well. He had brought his tool kit, thinking a shelf had broken.

By the time we got there, Roland was rubbing his knee, looking upset. Marissa was still on the ground.

"What the fuck happened here?" I asked, puzzled and more than just a little concerned. "Did you two get into a fight?"

"Not quite, although it was tempting!" exclaimed Roland. "I was here taking the pictures we'd talked about when she snuck up and startled the hell out of me. Seriously, this is insane! I really hurt my knee and I can barely stand."

I'd never seen Roland so angry. I put my hand on his shoulder and said, "I am so sorry. Let me get you an ice pack and I'd be glad to drive you home tonight. Let's try to make it over to the couch. Can you manage?"

Meanwhile, Tony and Peter were devising the best strategy to lift Marissa off the floor with minimal damage, although no doubt, they were tempted to leave her there, just a wee bit longer.

17

The Birthday Gift

We had a birthday tradition at the office: Whenever a team member celebrated a milestone birthday, we all chipped in towards a gift and organized a team dinner on the town.

Marissa's 40th was weeks away and Amanda, who loved shopping, volunteered to pick up a present. Team members agreed on a sum of $15 per person and, since there were 20 of us, we felt it was adequate. The money raised went towards a gift, a card and the dinner of the birthday boy or girl.

Amanda spent a whole weekend looking for the perfect gift that would appease Marissa. Buying gifts for others is never an easy task, but throw Marissa into the mix and be prepared for Mission Impossible.

Alas, Amanda found it! She came by my office and showed me the lovely necklace she'd bought. It was beautifully crafted and elegant.

"Good job, Amanda. Thank you for all your trouble."

"There is only one problem," she said. "The necklace was quite expensive and there is no money left to pay for her dinner. I'm really not comfortable asking the team to pitch in more money, since they are still recovering from Christmas expenses."

This has happened in the past and, honestly, I didn't mind. "I will take care of her dinner, so don't worry about it," I reassured Amanda.

The big day arrived, accompanied by a nasty snowstorm and temperatures way, way below zero. A perfect day for a celebration of this kind — or, perhaps it was an omen.

Marissa campaigned for weeks to ensure we picked the 'right' restaurant, because clearly, none of us were capable of making a good choice. She bluntly dismissed all the options we proposed and suggested her new favourite Italian restaurant, totally out of everyone's way and even more challenging to reach in a snowstorm. Within 30 minutes, everyone was there sporting long, tired faces.

Marissa was beaming. She was giggling and chatty, and even exchanged pleasantries and laughed at jokes, much to everyone's astonishment. (Every time she turned her head to chat with Roland, who was seated next to her, Tony would fill up her glass and wink at me.) I had committed to driving her home, so 'drink away', I thought to myself. Tipsy Marissa is far more agreeable than ordinary nutty Marissa, so Tony's 'secret' was very safe with me.

It was dessert time, finally! Marissa grilled the poor waiter. She had him recite every option on the dessert menu, apparently needing added assurance that each one was fresh. Fuck! Finally choosing a dark chocolate cake topped with ice-cream, she devoured it with immense pleasure, down to the last crumb.

"Was it good?" I asked.

"So, so," she replied.

As the table was being cleared, Amanda handed Marissa a beautiful gift bag, decorated by our very talented Annie, followed by a totally out of tune 'happy birthday' sung by all of us.

After a brief scan of the card, signed by the team, she unwrapped the gift and uttered: "Oh, this is so beautiful. Thank you so much. I really like it."

"We are happy you like it," I replied. "And a big 'thank you' to Amanda, who spent days shopping for the perfect gift." Everyone raised a glass to Amanda.

Mission accomplished, or so we thought.

Time flies. Ten years passed, and Marissa's 50th birthday was right around the corner.

I chatted with Amanda over a smoke in the parking lot, but neither one of us could come up with a suitable idea. As we made our way back, Marissa was getting out of her car and motioned

at me to wait for her. Amanda went ahead as I, reluctantly, waited for Marissa to waddle over.

"Do you have a few minutes? Can I talk to you?" she asked.

Fuck, I thought, what now? "Well, do you want to talk here in the parking lot, or should we go up to my office?"

"Here is good. This is a little embarrassing," she said with a failed attempt at a smile. "My birthday is coming up and I have a feeling the team will be buying a gift for me."

"Right, that is the plan, and you have a pretty big one coming up." I continued: "Is there a problem?"

"It's just, well, you know the gift I received for my 40th birthday, that necklace?" Her face frowned as she emphasized 'that necklace'.

"Yes, that lovely necklace that you said you liked so much. What about it?"

"Well, the thing is, I kind of hated it. I never wore it. It's really not my style."

"Seriously, you hated it? I can't believe this. So, all the excitement you displayed at the restaurant was a mere show? If you disliked it so much, we could have had it exchanged for something else. Why didn't you say something 10 bloody years ago? Just for the record Marissa, that was an expensive necklace and way over our budget." I was overtly annoyed.

"I didn't want to hurt anyone's feelings, but what can I say? I really don't like it. So, I was thinking, if the team is planning to buy me a gift for my upcoming birthday, there is something I really, really like."

Unbelievable, I thought. Only Marissa could have the nerve!

"What did you have in mind?" I asked with little enthusiasm.

"Well, there is this really nice tote bag I saw. It's a little expensive, but I can pay the difference if it's an issue."

"I see, send me a picture, please, and let me chat with the team. Here is a thought: Since you dislike the necklace, how about you gift it to Amanda?"

Her eyes widened with astonishment. "Give it to Amanda? But that was my gift!"

"Yes, it was your gift, but one you dislike and never wore."

"Sorry, I already gave it to my niece and she really likes it. Please don't tell them about the necklace. I feel badly about it. I saw it in a catalogue, and I know it was costly."

I was put off by this, certainly, but went to find Amanda once I was inside.

"Hey, Amanda, got a minute?"

"Sure, I'll be right over."

I recounted the awkward situation...

"I can't believe it! She actually told you what she wants us to buy her? Come to think of it, I never saw her wear the necklace. She is really something, isn't she?"

Just as Amanda was heading out, I received an email from Marissa.

"Don't leave, Amanda. Come see this."

"Oh, my God, is she out of her mind? This is a Kate Spade tote bag and they are very expensive. I can't believe she expects us to buy it. I'm sorry, but I can't afford to pay any extra right now and I am not comfortable asking the team. This is way, way out of our budget."

"I agree, Amanda. That was my initial reaction too, but keep in mind, she most likely won't be here for her 60th. This would be the very last gift we get her and that must be worth something, right?"

At that point, there were only 11 of us at the office, as some of the operation had moved over to head office. The team had agreed to up the budget to $20 per person a few years before, but even at that, we would be around $100 short — even without including her meal.

"Fuck it, Amanda. I will add the difference, but let's cancel the restaurant. We'll just get a cake and serve it mid-afternoon."

"Are you sure? That's a big difference to have to pay. I can't afford it, but it doesn't seem right for you to pay it all. You also contributed a large sum for that damned necklace. This is very upsetting."

"It is upsetting indeed, but this is Marissa, the gift that keeps on giving. Under different circumstances I would agree, but, hey: it's very likely her very last birthday with us and, for this alone, I'm willing to pay!"

18

Oh Please,
Not You Again?!

I was at our New York office, getting ready for an important meeting with a customer that wasn't too pleased with our recent performance. There had been delays with their orders and, although many issues were out of our control, such as delays at Customs, I had to deliver a plan of action and get them on board once again.

Their director, Joanne, was my least favourite customer — possibly of my entire career. Our conversations were entirely predictable. I would start by asking, politely and with a smile, "How are you doing today?" To which she would reply, with a deep sigh, "Ohhh, I could use a drink." She was generally miserable and unpleasant, and I'd had the 'pleasure' of working with her for over seven years, during which time she had nine different assistants come and go.

That morning, I had a great workout session, I was relaxed and mentally prepared to face Joanne and her team.

I arrived an hour early to ensure the boardroom was in order and that all the printed materials were neatly organized. Joanne and four of her associates arrived half an hour early. She appeared put off, as if she had hoped to catch me off guard. Bitch.

I wore one of my 'power' suits: a flattering and well-tailored grey suit, specifically chosen for this meeting.

All considered, the meeting was progressing well. Everyone seemed focused and engaged. Most were pleased with our proposed plan of action. Except for Joanne. Her contribution consisted of a sigh, followed by, "I am not loving it." The exchange of 'what the fuck' glances amongst her teammates was my cue to simply ignore her comment and move on. She was not pleased, but honestly, we had all heard her say similar words many times in past meetings.

After a three hour-long meeting, we decided to break for lunch, which I had ordered from a caterer. Just as I sat down, Anette, the office manager, came in and whispered in my ear: "Marissa is on the phone. She is very agitated. I could not make out what she was on about, but is there any chance you could talk to her? It's the third time she's called this morning."

Bloody hell!

I excused myself and stepped out of the boardroom.

"Yes, Marissa, this had better be very important. You do know that I am meeting with Joanne today, right?"

"I know, but I figured you would take a break at some point. This is important."

"Go on, then, but please make it short. We are taking a lunch break and will resume the meeting in 30 minutes."

"OK, well, we have a real problem here and I don't think I should address it. She reports to you, so I think it should come from you."

"OK, cut to the chase, please. Who is 'she' and what has she done? This had better be important and not another issue of crumbs on the kitchen table."

"It's not about Molly, it's Rachel, and I think it's very inappropriate for an office environment. It's rude and selfish."

"Marissa, get to the point, please, or it will have to wait until next week when I am back at the office. What has Rachel done to upset you?"

"It's not just me. I think everyone is upset. You see, she decided to take her lunch break at her cubicle and, while she was eating, she started applying nail polish. It's not right. It stinks and now the whole office stinks of nail polish too. She shouldn't do it at the office. It's very inconsiderate."

"Oh, my God. You have got to be fucking kidding me! Nail polish? This is the pressing issue that couldn't wait? Do you realize how absurd this conversation is? Did you talk to her at all?"

"Well, no, I thought you should. She does not report to me. You have to understand, the smell is very offensive. I am not making this up. Ask anyone."

Nutcracker!

"I have to go, Marissa. I will be at the office next Monday."

"So, wait, are you not going to talk to her today?"

I slammed the receiver, perhaps a little too hard, as it really startled Anette.

I called good old Tony and briefed him on the insane conversation.

"I can't believe she called you. We told her we didn't mind and, honestly, no one was bothered by it. It's Rachel. You know we all love her. She's going to an engagement party right after work. By the way, Marissa is storming out of the office as we speak. Oh boy, if looks could kill… Don't worry about this. She's just having one her nutty days."

I snuck out through the back door for a quick smoke. I thought about Joanne's strained demeanor. I couldn't remember the last time I'd seen her smile a genuine smile. Then I thought of Marissa's latest rant and burst out laughing. Calls me in middle of a big meeting to discuss nail polish. Un-fucking-believable! On days like this, retirement sounded heavenly.

The following Monday, back at the office, I went to the lunchroom to brew a cup of coffee. Rachel, Tony and Amanda were there.

"Good morning, all! Hey, Rachel, I like your nails, very nice!"

I winked at her and we all had a much-needed Monday morning laugh.

19

Sharing Platters

Our company had introduced a great incentive to boost morale and productivity. If in any given year the company met or exceeded sales goals, employees received a generous bonus to thank them for their contributions. Also, to celebrate the occasion, we went out to dinner at a restaurant chosen by the team.

For this year's outing, we were going to a well-known Greek restaurant, recommended by Roland. The restaurant had great reviews. We had to book a table a week in advance.

Marissa surprised us all when she announced she'd be joining us. She usually ignored team outings, other than the occasional Christmas party. With mixed emotions and a great deal of skepticism, we carpooled to the restaurant. Still, we were determined to enjoy the evening.

The waiter showed us to our table. There were 16 of us, so they set us up in one of the private rooms. Good call, I thought, since the team tends to get loud after the second round of drinks.

The waiter came to see us: "Good evening, ladies and gentlemen! My name is George. Is this your first visit to our restaurant?" he asked.

We all nodded, except for Roland, who raised his hand: "I've heard great things about this place, but haven't eaten here yet."

"Well, then, welcome! Let me explain briefly how it works. All of our dishes are served on large platters. You may order anything from the menu and we will keep the platters coming until you let us know you're ready for dessert."

There was such a variety of dishes and it would be nice to sample different ones. We all thought this sounded great. Of course, 'all' was a bit of an overstatement: Marissa was here to dampen the mood.

"Sharing platters? Yikes, that's disgusting. Why don't we each order our own plate?"

"Because, Marissa, this is how this restaurant operates, and, trust me, the food is spectacular. There is something here for everyone: beef, lamb, seafood, sides, you name it. You won't be disappointed, I promise," Tony said.

"Well, I am not so sure. I am really, really not crazy about sharing platters and I wish I would have known in advance."

"Have you been tested recently?" asked Tony, who was a little giddy already.

"Tested for what? What are you talking about?" she sneered.

"Drop it," I said, as I gently kicked Tony's leg under the table, trying hard to hold back my laughter. "Let's enjoy ourselves. We are here to celebrate."

Three waiters were busy placing platters on our table. Everything looked inviting and the aromas were mouth-watering. Everyone's eyes glowed with anticipation and only Marissa sat quietly, lips puckered in distaste, looking like a mock-up of an inflamed hemorrhoid.

"OK, everyone's been served? Let's dig in. *Bon Appetit* and enjoy!" I said, briefly turning my head towards Marissa and noticing she had filled her plate up after all.

The food was truly delicious. The meats and shrimp were grilled to perfection, emitting scents of olive oil, garlic, lemon and rosemary. I hadn't realized how hungry I was.

The waiters were attentive. As soon as they spotted an empty platter, they brought a new one. The grilled calamari dish was a hit, especially with Tony and Amanda. As soon as the waiter placed the second platter of calamari on the table, Amanda reached for it and started piling some on her plate. Just as the fork touched her lips...

"What are you doing? You don't have to be such a pig! These are sharing platters, you know. There are other people here and you should at least wait until everyone helps themselves!"

You guessed right: Marissa.

Poor Amanda. With her hand now trembling, the piece of calamari flew off her fork and landed on Roland's lap.

"Oh, my God, I am so sorry everyone. I didn't realize and it is just so good. I'm really sorry, but I just wanted a second helping. I can put it back..."

"Nonsense, Amanda. Eat as much as you feel like. Besides, look around: most of us aren't even eating calamari, so please enjoy it." Her face was red with embarrassment and I felt badly for her.

Although I was already full, I decided to take some more of the calamari to ease the tension, for Amanda's sake.

I called the waiter and whispered in his ear. A few minutes later, he came to our table with yet another large platter of calamari, picked up Marissa's plate, and placed the mound of seafood right in front of her.

Her eyes nearly popped right out.

"What are you doing? I didn't order this! I don't eat calamari. Take it away from me. I hate the smell!" said Marissa, as she aggressively pushed the platter away.

The waiter looked at me, confused.

"Oh, I ordered it for you Marissa. I just wanted to make sure you don't leave here feeling short-changed." I raised my glass: "Cheers everyone," I said, with a smile.

20

Marissa:
A Survival Guide

New employees were often perplexed by Marissa. Senior employees 'got used' to her somewhat, although now and then they still took a blow when their guard was down.

A former employee once suggested that there should be a 'how to' guide to help employees manage challenging Marissa mishaps. I often thought we should put it into action. If anything, it would give them a bit of an edge — not to mention inject subtle humour into these bizarre confrontations.

Tony, Roland, Amanda and I have been here the longest and have witnessed countless 'Marissa signature moments' over the years. They loved the idea of putting together a Marissa survival guide and were eager to get started. We decided to meet at Gambino's for food and drinks, and to work on it together.

We arrived around 6 pm, ordered our meals and drinks,

and eagerly embarked on our unique project. Three hours later—after lots of laughter, raw profanity and two bottles of wine—we'd hashed out an initial draft.

Title:	**A survival guide for beginners**
User manual:	How to soften the blow?
Subject matter:	Marissa, the one and only
Description:	Short and stubby with unusually large feet
Distinguishing feature:	Crazy eyes
What she likes most:	Meat pies, bacon, hot dogs, cookies, chocolate, good hair days, flattery and gossip
Dislikes intensely:	Mushrooms, tomatoes, fish, most dairy foods and all sorts of people
Known phobias:	Arachnophobia, claustrophobia, entomophobia and Brumotactillophobia
Firm belief:	I am so smart; this company won't last without me!

There will be times, many times, when you will be confronted head on by this woman. Don't despair, because we're here to help!

Helpful tips:

The following tips have been tested and proven useful. They will help you steer clear of the lunacy of dealing with Marissa:

Rule no. 1:   Do not engage.

Rule no. 2:   Stay calm.

Rule no. 3:   Breathe, breathe, breathe.

Rule no. 4:   Always keep a small stash of cookies and chocolates handy.

Rule no. 5:   The battery-operated spider may be used if all else fails!

When confronted by Marissa:

To further illustrate some combat and defense tactics, we've provided examples of a few real-life Marissa strikes, with possible responses that are guaranteed to throw her off balance. These defence strategies can be easily adapted to various strikes.

Special Note: Like a bee, our office Queen B is best managed with a spoonful of honey.

Here we go:

She shoots:

She barges into your office and tosses a folder on your desk containing a report you worked hard to complete. "This is crap, you completely missed the point!" she shouts.

You retaliate:

Breathe, stay calm, put on your most disarming smile and respond: "Wow, Marissa, that is a gorgeous blouse. Is it new? It looks great on you."

She shoots:

She hounds you as you come out of the bathroom: "You left a dirty plate in the sink. It's disgusting. Why can't you wash it right away?"

You retaliate:

"Oh, there was a big hairy spider on the kitchen counter and I'm waiting for it to crawl away..."

Pause and prepare for a frantic screech.

She shoots:

You've just arrived at the office and have barely had a chance to make it to your desk: "Do you really think you should be wearing this dress?" she says. "It's too tight and short, and I don't think you should wear it at the office!"

You retaliate:

"Hey, look, I was over at the Lindt store on Sunday. Got you your favourite chocolates. Here, take one. What the heck, take the whole packet."

She shoots:

She catches you approaching the thermostat and bolts towards you: "Can't you read the sign? Don't touch the thermostat! I am too hot."

You retaliate:

"Oh, Marissa, good morning. Wow, did you just get a new hairdo? Looks great, very flattering."

She shoots:

You are all in the lunchroom. Marissa is there as well, devouring her lunch in silence. She keeps staring at you with her crazy eyes, her face turning red and puffy. She suddenly raps her fork on the table and hollers at you: "Must you laugh so loudly?"

You retaliate:

Reach into your lunch bag, take out the packet of cookies and hand it to her on a napkin (note: always hand it on a napkin, never with bare hands!).

"Here, Marissa, I went shopping yesterday and saw your favourite cookies. Go ahead, help yourself. Have one or four.

Important:

In order to keep this guide current, please report any 'shooting incidents' as they happen and we'll update it promptly.

Remember, she has her good moments now and then, so enjoy them while they last!

Hope you have enjoyed
Marissa's signature moments!

Acknowledgements

I am grateful for the superb team that guided me:

Nicolette Little, for her publishing and copy-editing support

David Moratto, for his creative book design

My son, for his love and encouragement and, most wicked sense of humour.

About the author

Elena spent her entire career as an executive in the corporate world. Well travelled and has lived in various countries around the world.